Lincoln Township Library
206?? W. John Beers Rd.
??sville, MI 49122
??29-9575

D1537545

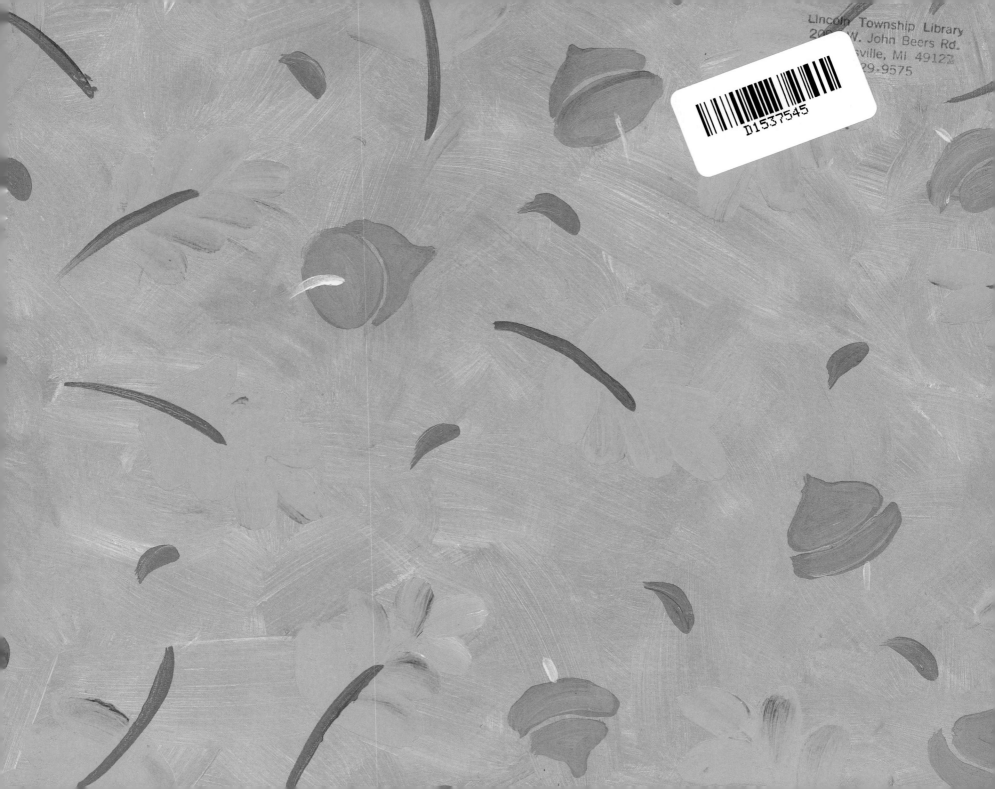

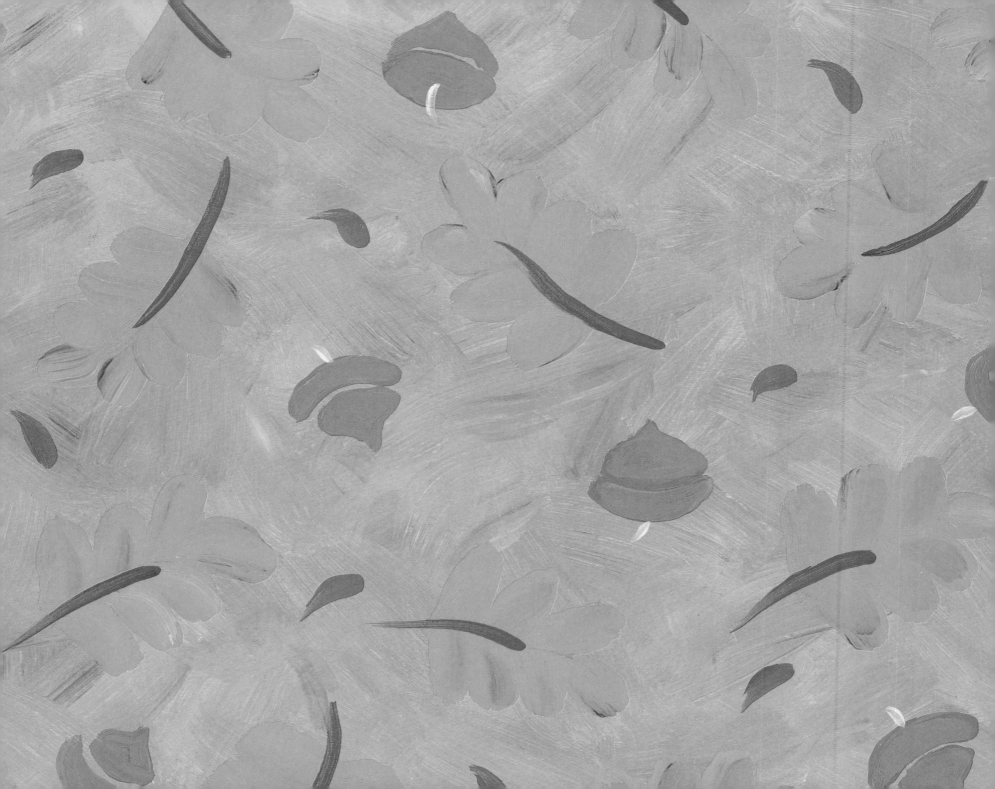

# BRAVERY SOUP

## by Maryann Cocca-Leffler

Lincoln Township Library
2099 W. John Beers Rd.
Stevensville, MI 49127
429-9575

Albert Whitman & Company
Morton Grove, Illinois

Also by Maryann Cocca-Leffler:

**JUNGLE HALLOWEEN**

**MISSING: ONE STUFFED RABBIT**

**MR. TANEN'S TIES**

Library of Congress Cataloging-in-Publication Data

Cocca-Leffler, Maryann, 1958–
  Bravery soup / written and illustrated by Maryann Cocca-Leffler.
    p. cm.
      Summary: Carlin, who is frightened by everything, wants to try some of
      Big Bear's Bravery Soup, but first he must travel through a dark forest to
      a monster's cave to retrieve an important ingredient.
      ISBN 0-8075-0870-5
        [1. Fear — Fiction. 2. Bears — Fiction.] I. Title.  PZ7.C638 Br 2002  [E] — dc21
      2001004167

Text and illustrations copyright © 2002 by Maryann Cocca-Leffler.
Published in 2002 by Albert Whitman & Company, 6340 Oakton Street,
Morton Grove, Illinois 60053-2723.
Published simultaneously in Canada by General Publishing, Limited, Toronto.
All rights reserved. No part of this book may be reproduced or transmitted
in any form or by any means, electronic or mechanical, including photocopying,
recording, or by any information storage and retrieval system, without
permission in writing from the publisher.
Printed in China through Colorcraft Ltd, Hong Kong.
10  9  8  7  6  5  4  3  2  1

The paintings are rendered in acrylic.
For more information about Albert Whitman & Company,
visit our web site at www.albertwhitman.com.
For more information about Maryann Cocca-Leffler,
visit her web site at www.maryanncoccaleffler.com.

In memory of my dear friend Marcia Sommers,
who taught me about bravery.

Carlin was afraid of everything.
He was afraid of bumps in the night,

BUMP

of trying new things,

SWIMMING

of being alone.

He was afraid of his own shadow!

"You need a bit of bravery," said his friend Zack, "and I know where you can get it."

Early the next morning Zack led Carlin to the edge of the woods.
There they saw Big Bear, the bravest animal in all the land.
He was standing by the fire, stirring a big pot of soup.

"So you want some bravery, do you?" asked Big Bear.

"Y-y-yes," stammered Carlin.

"Well, I'm mixing up a batch of Bravery Soup right here, but I'm missing an important ingredient. Will you get it for me?" asked Big Bear.

"Will it make me brave?" asked Carlin.

"Most certainly," said Big Bear. "But your journey will not be easy. You must go, alone, through the Forbidden Forest to Skulk Mountain. On the mountaintop you will see a cave. In the cave you will find a box. Bring that box to me."

Carlin gasped.

## "ALONE? THE FOREST? THE CAVE?"

His knees were shaking.

"You are braver than you think," said Big Bear.

When the animals heard that Carlin was venturing
into the Forbidden Forest alone, they gathered around him.

"Here is a basket of
food. The forest is full of
poisonous plants."

"Here is armor to protect
you from the wild beasts."

"Here is a raft to cross
the raging river."

"Here is a big stick to fight the fierce monster that lives in the cave."

**"WILD BEASTS? POISON? RAGING RIVER? FIERCE MONSTER?"**

Carlin's whole body shuddered. Then he remembered Big Bear's words: "You are braver than you think."

"Now or never," Carlin thought.
Slowly, he walked into the thick forest.

His friends waited for a while, growing
more and more worried.

"It is much too dangerous for little Carlin,"
they said. They decided to search for him.

As Carlin's friends entered the forest, they came across the armor.

"OH!

HE IS HURT!"

They found the basket of food, untouched.

"OH, MY!

HE IS STARVING!"

Then they spotted the raft,
floating at the river's edge.

"OH, NO!
THE RIVER HAS SWEPT HIM AWAY!"

But Carlin was not hurt.
He had soon realized that he could not walk fast
wearing the heavy armor.
"I can flee the beasts more quickly
without it," he thought. So he took
the armor off.

Carlin was not starving.
As he walked along, he noticed animals and birds
feasting on fruits in the Forbidden Forest.
He saw some strawberries. "I can eat these!"
he thought. So he dropped his heavy basket
and ate the delicious fruit.

Carlin had not been swept away.
When he came to the raging river, he found that a tree lay over the water.
He tossed the raft aside. Carefully, he began to make his
way across. He took one tiny step and then
another, until finally he reached
the other side.

# "I DID IT!"

he cheered.

Carlin looked up.
There before him was
Skulk Mountain.

Carlin trudged on. The mountain
was covered with thick bushes and vines.
He broke his stick cutting a path.
Then he spotted giant footprints!
Carlin had discovered the
monster's cave.

Trembling, he entered.

Minutes later, his friends found the broken stick by the mouth of the cave.

"OH, NO! HE HAS BEEN EATEN BY THE MONSTER!"

But Carlin had not been eaten by the monster.
He peered into the cave and squinted his eyes. There, on the ground,
was the box! Just then, something moved from the shadows.

## THE MONSTER!

Terrified, Carlin hid behind a pile
of rocks. Suddenly, one of the
rocks tumbled over!

The sound made the monster jump and howl!

"Who is it?" he whimpered. **"WHAT D-D-DO YOU WANT?"**

Carlin had cast a long, spooky shadow.

"Could this scary monster be afraid of **ME?**" he thought.

"My name is Carlin," Carlin said in his deepest,
loudest voice. "I came for the box."

"This box?" The monster tossed the box
towards Carlin. "Take it!" he said.

"Just please don't hurt me!"

Carlin grabbed the box and ran from the cave . . . bumping right into his friends.

"RUN! THE MONSTER!"

They all raced down the mountain,

over the river,
through the forest,

and back to the edge
of the woods.

At last, the tired animals gathered around Big Bear's fire. Carlin carried the precious box.

"Now it is time," said Big Bear.
"Open the box."
Carlin pried off the lid.

# THE BOX WAS EMPTY!

Carlin was sad. "I'm sorry, Big Bear. I didn't get the secret ingredient for bravery."

"But you did," said Big Bear with a smile.
"The box was always empty."
"Do you mean my journey was for **NOTHING?**"
asked Carlin in surprise.
"Your journey was not for nothing,"
said Big Bear. "You faced the forest and
you faced your fear. It is not what is inside
the **BOX** that makes bravery. It is what is
inside of **YOU!**"
"So what about the Bravery Soup?"
asked Carlin.
"It's called Bravery Soup because
I only serve it to the brave!"
said Big Bear.

# "I AM BRAVE!"

said Carlin.

And he held up his bowl.

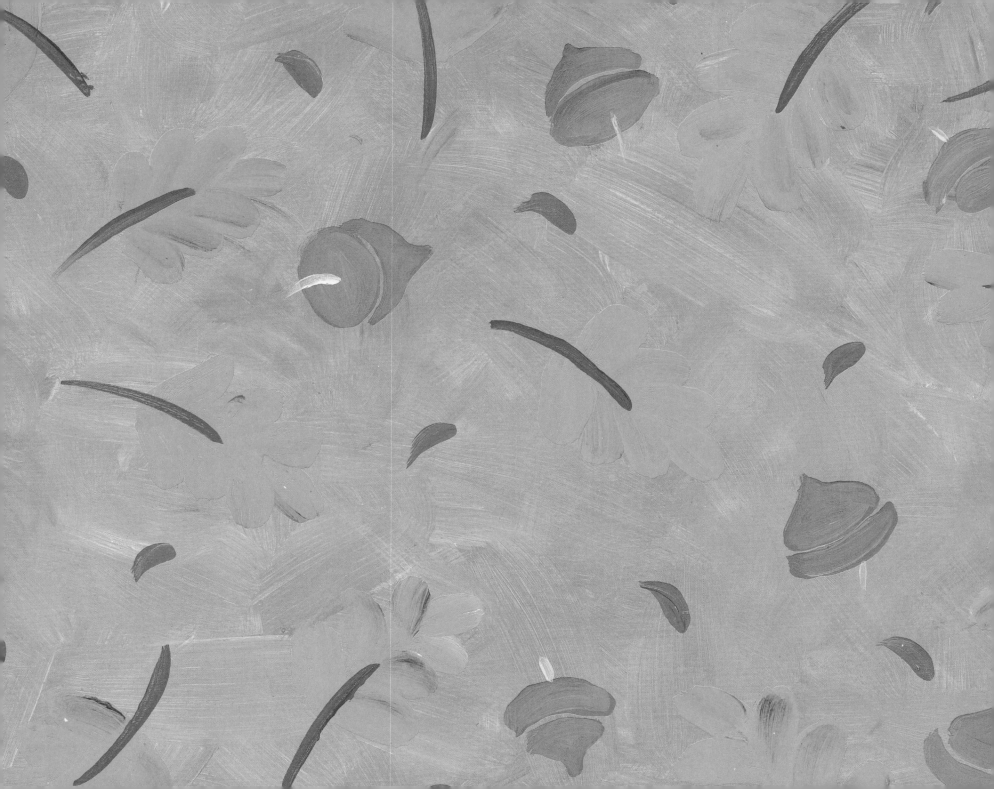

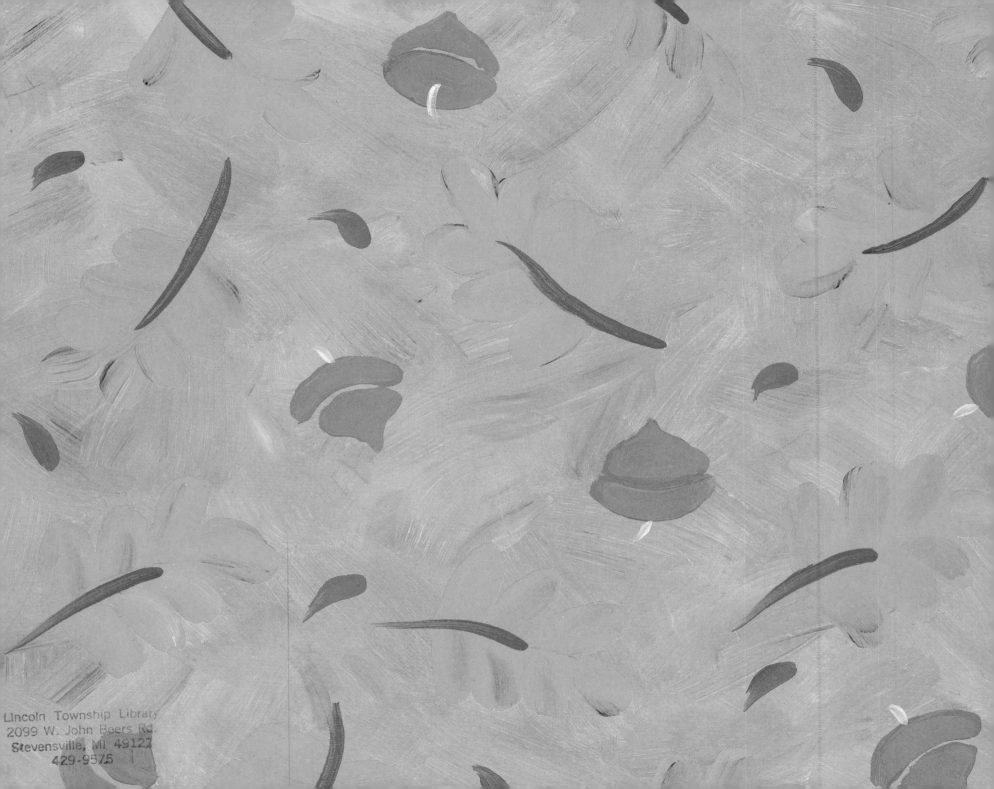

Lincoln Township Library
2099 W. John Beers Rd.
Stevensville, MI 49127
429-9575